THE HOUR GLASS

THE HOUR GLASS

Sixty Fables for This Moment in Time

by Carl Japikse

Illustrated by Mark Peyton

ARIEL PRESS
The Publishing House of Light
Columbus, Ohio

Third Printing

This book is made possible by a gift to the Publications Fund of Light from Judith Renaud Ross

THE HOUR GLASS
Copyright © 1984 by Light

All Rights Reserved. No part of this book may be used or reproduced in any manner whatsoever without written permission, except in the case of brief quotations embodied in articles and reviews. Printed in the United States of America. Direct inquiries to: Ariel Press, 3854 Mason Road, Canal Winchester, Ohio 43110. No royalties are paid on this book.

ISBN 0-89804-045-0

Library of Congress Card Catalog Number: 83-70304

TO ROSE

"To dazzle let the Vain design;
To raise the Thought, and touch the Heart be thine!"

PREFACE

Long, long ago, there lived a pig who did not act piggish. He was refined and cultured, read a lot of good books, and stoutly refused to eat garbage or leftovers. His taste ran more to French cooking.

In that same era, there was also a lion who was not in the least interested in being a tyrant of the jungle. He much preferred writing love poetry and composing songs. Calves lay alongside him without fear.

The pig and the lion were friends of an honest fox, called frequently on a wolf with the most charming manners, played cards with a shy, retiring bluejay, dined on weekends with a vegetarian snake, supported the political activities of an ombudsman ostrich, and greatly admired the genuine religious piety of a mystical weasel.

I had hoped these animals would be the characters of my fables. But the Muses decreed otherwise. I was stuck instead with a group of greedy, thieving, murderous, proud, self-righteous, nearsighted, narrow-minded, callous, scheming, stupid, effete, and arrogant *beasts*.

There are even a few stories about people.

THE HOUR GLASS

ONCE UPON A TIME

Once upon a time, there was no time. It was just a possibility in the imagination of the Sun. But the Sun shines without regard to time, so he never bothered to create it.

On Earth, however, the plants and animals needed time. They were waiting to evolve and grow.

Without the seasons, the plants did not know when to break forth from the soil and begin a new cycle of growth. So they had to remain seeds.

Without the day and the night, the animals did not know when to rest and when to be active. They resembled stuffed toys more than living, breathing animals.

But the impulse to grow is a mighty force, so strong not even the absence of time can hold it back. It rose up in rebellion, and the plants and animals of earth cried forth to the Sun:

"Give us time!"

In that moment—the first moment—time was born. Growth began. And with every turn of the hour glass since, the imagination of the Sun has been enriched.

THE BRIDGE

An old farmer called to him his two sons. "Instead of dividing the farm, I will bequeath my entire property to the one of you who first completes a simple test. I wish to build a bridge across the lower gully and need stone for the piles. The first of you to gather twenty tons of rock shall receive my inheritance."

The older son set off immediately for the quarry and began hauling back loads of stone in a wheelbarrow. Day after day he labored, and slowly his pile grew in size. His brother, meanwhile, did nothing but relax in the shade, drinking his father's wine and humming songs.

When the older had gathered ten tons, he asked his idle brother: "Don't you care about Father's inheritance?"

"Sure I care," said the younger. "How far along are you?"

"I've collected ten tons," his brother replied proudly. "You'll never catch up with me." The other smiled, and each day after that inquired how his brother's work progressed.

Finally the day arrived when the older son announced he would finish by nightfall. The younger arched his brow. "Oh? Then it is time for me to start." He set aside his wineskin and climbed the high cliff opposite the gully. On top were a number of large boulders. With a pole he had cut on the way, the youth dislodged one and sent it tumbling to the rocks below. As it struck, the boulder shattered into dozens of basket-sized stones. He did the same with the other boulders, then went to call his father.

"Upon the fulcrum of my mind," he said, "I have built my bridge to your legacy. And my brother need not labor any more, for I shall share it with him."

THE FISH OF GOD

Experience is not always a reliable teacher.

A fish was caught by a fisherman one day, only to be thrown back into the water because he was too small. Alarmed at first by his near encounter with death, the fish soon became ecstatic, believing himself the beneficiary of a "divine deliverance." Not understanding the reason why he had been spared, he concluded that the entire episode had been a test of his spirituality—a test he had passed triumphantly. Moreover, he decided that only a fish who had endured such a test could truly be considered a "fish of God."

He therefore sought out his friends and related his experience. "I have been blessed by divine providence," he proclaimed, "lifted into the heavens and then sent back into the waters. You, too, should undergo the test I have passed; you should subject yourself to the trial of the hook. To be a complete fish, you must prove the purity of your piscience."

The other fish accepted his story without question and swam off eagerly, in search of a heavenly fishing line to bite. Unfortunately, they were all larger than their friend the prophet, and never returned.

The fish who had been thrown back lived into dignified old age—but he lived alone.

A SILLY NOTION

Two pups romped through the countryside, their first time outside the city. So much exercise soon made them thirsty. "Oh, I wish our masters were close by to give us a dish of water," yapped one.

Shortly the pair passed a cool spring bubbling from the ground. "What's this?" asked the second.

The other went up to the spring, sniffed it, then tasted it with his tongue. "It's water!" he shouted.

"It can't be," his friend barked back. "There isn't a man making it."

"But it *is* water," the first insisted, "and a lot fresher than what we get in our own dishes."

THE CLIMB TO THE TOP

At the very top of a high cliff lived an eagle. Throughout the woods below, the eagle was known as a bothersome fop, always boasting how he lived higher than everyone else. He pestered the animals while they worked and bragged that he was the only bird or beast ever to reach the summit of the cliff.

One day on returning to his hideaway, the eagle was astonished to find a snail awaiting him. "What are you doing here, slug?" the eagle cried, bewildered. "How did *you* manage to climb to the top?"

The snail glanced back on the silvery path he had left and smiled. "I rose," he said, "by dragging myself through the dirt."

12.

A LA CARTE

Throughout the centuries since Aesop told the first fable, countless crows have been tricked by as many foxes into forfeiting tidbits of meat and cheese. Finally, a crow determined to even the score. Procuring a scrap of red rubber at a junkyard, he carried it to his nest. When the next fox passed, the crow pulled out the decoy and began pecking at it.

The fox was nearsighted and thought the crow was lunching on a juicy morsel of meat. As his forefathers had before him, he decided to wheedle the snack from the crow. Launching into the traditional song and dance, he called out:

"Ah, Sir Crow, what a majestic bird you are, perched on your oaken standard and garbed in a robe of silky ebony. You must be the trumpeter of the king himself. I beg of you, Sir Herald—trill a few notes for me."

Heeding his cue, the crow dropped the piece of rubber and warbled out a few strained notes. The fox dashed over and greedily snatched up the abandoned tidbit. But when he tried to swallow it, he choked and gasped and spat the tasteless meal back out.

The crow flew alongside the retching fox and laughed with cruel amusement. "I can see you enjoyed the appetizer! Now, what will it be for the main course? May I suggest the chef's specialty: a nice, large slice of humble pie?"

The fox glowered at his tormentor. Then slowly, ever so slowly, a cunning smile of inspiration broke across his face. "I have a better idea," he said, grabbing the bird in his paws. "I shall eat crow."

IT HAS RISEN

The day he died, a master baker whispered to his son his secret recipe for bread. And thus the son's success was assured, for the bread was renowned throughout the province. His competitors, however, were distressed that the son was continuing the tradition of the father.

"It's not fair!" they argued. "We, too, gain our livelihood by baking bread for the people: the recipe should be made common knowledge for the benefit of all." So they filed suit in a local court to force the son to make the recipe public. By a quirk of justice, they won.

The son obeyed the court. But when the others tried his recipe, the yeast did not rise. They stormed back into court, protesting the son had deceived them.

"I will prove I have acted in good faith," the son said. He set up his equipment in the courtroom and began to mix a batch of dough according to the recipe. The other bakers watched closely. When he had finished kneading, he set the dough aside to rise. It proofed perfectly.

The son turned to the magistrate. "In addition to the recipe, my father left me the *right* to make this bread. As any baker knows, dough can never be forced to rise. It needs the proper atmosphere. In the same way, no "right" in this world can ever be grabbed forcibly. It must be given—and received—in the proper atmosphere."

AN ORDINARY MAN

A city installed a water fountain in its town hall. When the first person tried to use it, however, the fountain was dry. The company which installed the fountain was called in to repair it, yet no defect could be found. It was in perfect working condition. But no matter who tried it, no water came.

Word of the fountain which gave no water spread quickly, and jokes abounded about "typical government services." Eventually, the city stopped trying to get the fountain to work, and just let it be. But everyone who visited the town hall made a point of stopping by the fountain to get a drink—knowing they would not. The town became famous for it.

One day, a man who was pure of heart and wise in mind came to the city for a visit. Hearing of the fountain, he went to investigate this strange phenomenon for himself. But when he stepped up to it and pressed the lever, the fountain worked! He drank deeply and stepped back.

Naturally, the others in the building were amazed at this event, and immediately rushed to the fountain to be among the first to drink from it. But when they tried, the fountain stopped working again. None of them could get a drink. Finally, they called the man back. "Try it again," they cried.

He did—and once more the fountain flowed freely.

"Are you some kind of magician," a man in the crowd asked, "that you can make this fountain work?"

"No, it is life itself which is magical," the wise man replied. "This is just an ordinary fountain, as I am an ordinary man, but the water you seek is water that no city can supply for its people. It can only be found by each person on his or her own, by developing an unselfish heart and a noble mind. So stop looking for the city to quench your thirst."

And having explained the magic of the fountain, he cupped his hands to catch the water, and let everyone drink from what he had collected.

18.

THE WEB

A spider found refuge in the shadows of a little-used shed. There, from joist to stanchion to tamped dirt floor, he patiently spun his web. With slow precision he wove the fragile strands of spider-gauze—he, the weather-worn fisherman rigging his nets, the lighthearted beachcomber assembling his hammock, the architect transforming blueprints into steel and concrete.

A small rubber ball bounced into the shed and underneath the almost completed webbing. In close pursuit, a boy chased the ball inside, plunging into the unseen web. For a single moment all movement hung suspended in air; then, with arms flailing, the boy brushed the filaments from his face, pulling down the vectors, the parallels, the parabolas, the interstices, the spider.

From the floor the fallen spider surveyed the wispy superstructure strewn about him. The boy, retrieving the ball, raced back outside, calling to his playmate:

"Yuck! I got caught in a spider web."

THE GREAT SCHEME

King Lion commanded a lowly ass to accompany him on a hunting trip.

"Sit behind this blind," the lion instructed the donkey when they had reached a great meadow. "Wait fifteen minutes while I station myself, and then begin braying as loudly as you can. Your noise will scare the wild beasts, and in their fright they will be easy prey." The ass dutifully memorized the instructions, repeating them twice to be sure. Then the lion set off.

Which was silly, for donkeys cannot tell time. Only a few minutes had passed when the overeager assistant raised his head and commenced braying. The premature wailing caught the lion off his guard, and in his surprise he forgot it was only the whine of his ass. The great hunter panicked and fled the meadow.

And thus the animals of the forest were saved, not by their own resources but by an ass who was trusted by an even greater one.

MASTER AND SLAVE

A young man married the most beautiful woman in the village. On his wedding night, he sung to the champagne to bless their union.

Years later—when he had grown old—his wife died. He began drinking heavily of cheap wine, to dull his sorrow and feeling of loss. But time does not forget. The whole house—the walls, the furniture, and even the wine bottles themselves—shuddered to see this proud old man lose his grip on reality.

One night as he reached for a bottle of wine, the bottle reproached him: "Master! Master!"

The old man stopped short. He thought for a great while. At last, he answered. "You think me drunk," he said, "but I am sober enough to recognize sarcasm. And I am still young enough to recall singing to you in joy. So I shall drink to forget no more—only to remember and be thankful for the many blessings of my life."

And once again the bottle said, "Master, master"—but this time gently, and with a note of approval.

COLOR ME BRIGHT

When the birds were first created, all were colored dull brown. They carried a tune nicely, but were not much to look at.

The drab complexions of the birds disturbed Lion, king of all animals. Calling before him a peacock, Lion commissioned him to paint the birds of the world bright colors. The peacock was flattered by this command, but stammered, "Your Highness, I know nothing of painting."

"Well, learn!" roared Lion.

So the peacock learned. He journeyed down to the riverbank and began dabbling in the muds and clays along the water's edge. He mixed yellow and blue and compared it with the moss on the bank. He learned to thin his colors with water for smoother application. He developed a secret way of adding luster to his colors, so they would shine.

Finally, after much experimentation, he had perfected a technique. Under authority of Lion, he summoned the birds of the world one by one, to paint their feathers.

He started simply, coloring the raven black, the cardinal red. As he gained confidence, he became more creative, giving the flicker black speckles on a white breast with bold yellow wings, and creating a delicate show of miniature brilliance for the hummingbirds. By the time the peacock began working on the tropical birds, he had matured into a master artist.

When his task was completed, the peacock returned to the king. "Sire," he said, "your request has been fulfilled. All the birds have been colored."

"I have seen your work," replied Lion, "and it is very good. But you overlooked one bird."

"Which?" inquired the peacock.

"Yourself," the king responded. And, indeed, the peacock looked as drab as ever.

"Not true, not true," the peacock protested. "I finished myself just this morning." And spreading open his tail feathers, he revealed a subtlety of iridescence, an elegance of design far surpassing his earlier efforts.

"Self-portraits," the bird observed as he promenaded before his liege, "usually tend to be the artist's best work."

24.

FAIR WEATHER

No animal in the kingdom had a greater reputation for carefulness and mastery of his environment than a certain goat who lived high on a mountain. The reputation was well-deserved, too; his daily treks took him over the most treacherous terrain. One false step and he could fall thousands of feet. But he was sure of foot and famous for it.

Indeed, his fame became so great that many animals sought him out for advice on coping with the adverse aspects of environment. In time, he began conducting regular survival expeditions, wrote books on the subject, and became very popular among the young.

One day, as he was teaching a class in mountaineering, a fierce storm suddenly came up. The students were buffeted and battered by the wind and rain, but the goat resolutely led everyone to safety. Once back, one of his students was overcome with awe at the calm and self-assured way the goat had met the crisis.

"Oh, it's really not very difficult to make your way about the mountain in a storm such as this," the goat remarked. "The conditions are so unfavorable you have no choice but to keep yourself focused on the outer environment. The most dangerous time to be on the mountain is when the outer weather is fair. That's when the inner storms of your emotions and mind tend to mount; memories, worries, and daydreams rise within you. If you aren't careful then, you can easily be distracted—and forget what your feet are doing. Years ago, two of my friends fell to their deaths this very way."

"And what has spared you from the same fate?" the student asked.

"I have always saved my worries and daydreams for when I am not climbing mountains."

TO THE REAR, MARCH!

A rooster watched a turkey strut backwards across the barnyard, tripping over bumps and stumbling into troughs as he went. "Why are you walking backward?" the cock inquired. "It looks terribly awkward."

The turkey backed into a combine, cropping off his tail feathers. "I'm analyzing the past so I won't make the same mistakes twice."

A STRONG ATTACHMENT

A porpoise and her offspring were swimming alongside a large ship with thousands of barnacles encrusted on its hull.

"Are barnacles bad for the ship, Mama?" one of the young dolphins asked.

"Yes, indeed," his mother replied. "They slow it down and rob much of the strength of the iron."

"Can't the sailors knock off the barnacles?" asked another.

"They can, but it's very difficult, and often the barnacles tear out large hunks of metal as they are removed. Remember this lesson, for barnacles can cling to you, too, if you wander carelessly into their waters. If one should attach to you, swim for the strong currents before he is firmly set—for if you don't, you'll never shake him loose."

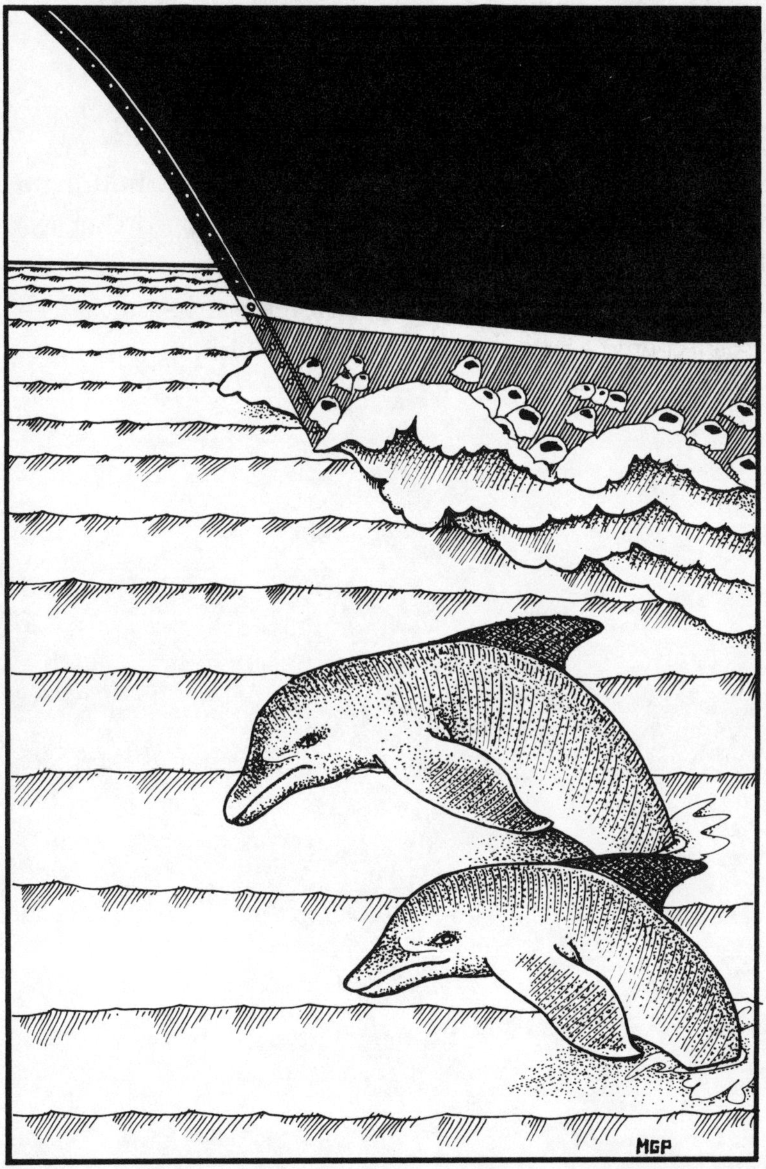
MGP

AMEN

A gnat alit on a page of the Word of God during a scripture lesson. Annoyed, the pastor snapped shut the book, squashing the insect.

Reopening the Bible, the minister brushed away the crushed gnat—and continued reading, without missing so much as the dot of an "i."

A NEW ANGLE

A many-sided polygon chanced to meet a simple straight line. "Oh, you poor thing," sneered the polygon with disdain. "How dreadfully dull life must be as a straight line! So undeveloped, so primitive, so rustic!"

The line said nothing, but slowly began to rotate about his midpoint. Gaining momentum, he spun himself into a perfect circle. Then, stretching and contracting his figure as he twirled, he transformed the circle into an ellipse, undulating like a belly dancer around the dazzled polygon. Suddenly the line stopped, and bending down, formed a right angle, then doubled up again to become a triangle. Straightening out into a line again, he concluded his performance by suspending himself like a hammock between two dots. Sagging there in mid-space, he was a perfect parabola.

"You see," said the line to the stunned polygon, "I am not lacking in talent. I could even contort myself into a bizarre-looking polygon such as yourself. But life is more rewarding as a simple, unpretentious line."

THE COMPASS

A foolish man had the habit of riding his donkey from town to town in a most peculiar manner: he never followed the straight roads, but always wandered erratically through the countryside, often covering two or three times the necessary distance. Many people laughed at him for this odd way of traveling—but then, what would one expect from a fool?

One day, a well-meaning friend offered the fool a compass. "This will help you find your direction, so you can travel in straight lines." To the friend's surprise, however, the foolish man refused the gift. The friend asked why.

"If I ever start traveling in straight lines," the fool replied simply, "people would stop thinking I was foolish."

33.

THE GREATEST SHOW ON EARTH

Burning clouds of crimson and sulfur burst into the night air. Aroused from sleep, the islanders looked to the sky: a distant volcano had erupted, belching out fire and lava, lighting the dark with an effulgent glow. The men and women watched, not in terror, for they were safe, but entranced by the brute beauty of the explosion.

As the first impact subsided, the islanders realized one old man had not been watching with them. "What did you see, compadre, of more interest than the volcano?" they asked.

"You," their friend replied. "All of you. The volcano explodes all night—I can watch it later. Your reactions, however, were of the moment only; I did not wish to miss them. For your faces erupted, too, like reflections of the fire. At first you were afraid, and your eyes darted back and forth, but the fear soon dissolved into peaceful reverence for the splendor of the night.

"Nature stages many spectacular shows, but none that compares with the drama in a man's eyes as he beholds the glory of the world."

MEASURING TAPE

A fat man weighing three hundred and sixty pounds purchased a fine cowhide belt. Some time later, he went on a diet to lose weight.

After losing sixty pounds, he said: "Well, I must not be fat anymore—I've taken in all the notches on my belt."

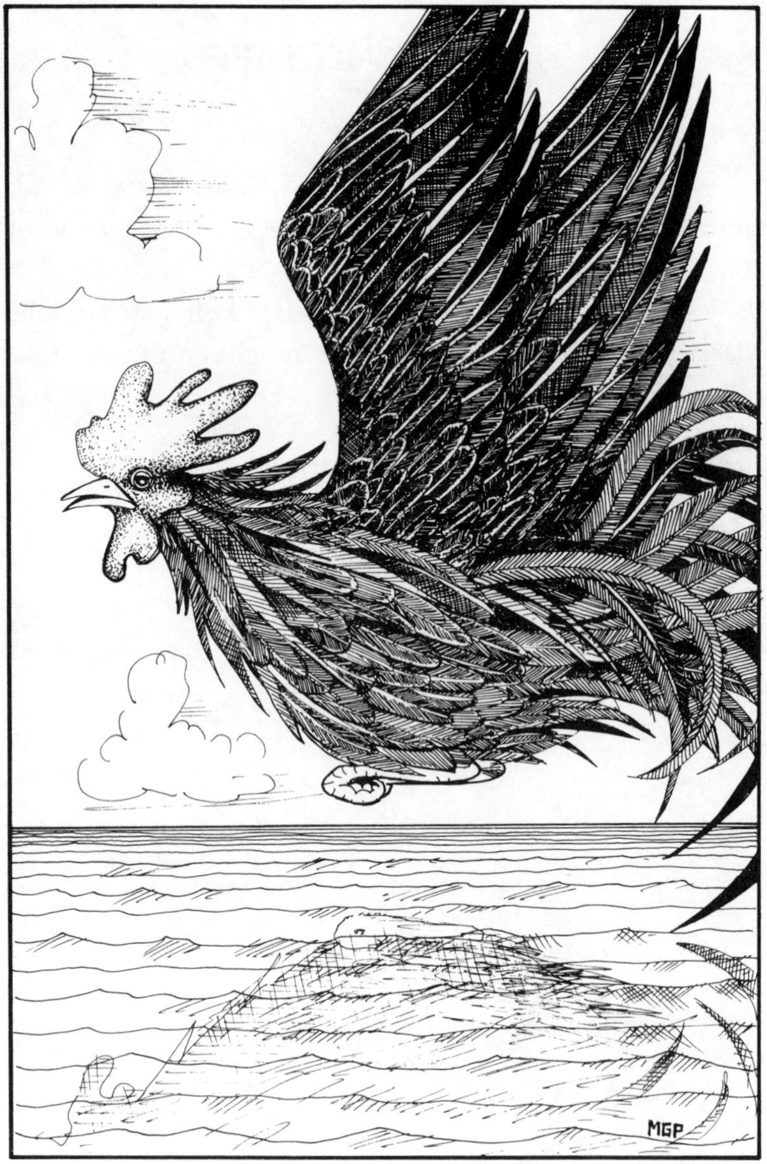
MGP

A FOWL STORY

Why can't a chicken fly? The true reason was known to Aesop, who told it in a fable.

In the early days of the animal kingdom, the chicken was an accomplished flier. He could fly faster and higher than other birds and perform fancy tricks, too. He took pride in his skills and often showed them off by flying sideways and upside-down and somersaulting in mid-air.

One day, as the chicken was flying over a lake, he spotted his reflection in the water below. "Oh, what a talented bird I am," he thought, and he began performing all the tricks he knew, to see them in the reflection. He was so busy admiring himself that he forgot everything else—and crashed into a tree on the edge of the pond. Stunned by the blow, he toppled to the ground unconscious. When he revived, not realizing what had occurred, he blamed the accident on the air.

"Why did you place an invisible wall in my path, Air?" the ruffled chicken demanded.

"I did no such thing," protested Air. "You struck the tree when you weren't looking."

"Don't lie," squawked the chicken. "Tree is my friend. He's not to blame—you're the culprit. You cannot be trusted any more."

"Ungrateful bird!" fumed Air. "You'll regret this false

accusation, for I shall having nothing more to do with you."

"Good!" cried the angry chicken.

"Well, just try flying without my support!" retorted Air. And he left in a huff.

The chicken did try. But no matter how much he flapped his wings, it was no use. He would rise a few feet off the ground, then plummet down in an awkward clump of feathers. He never flew again.

THE MUSIC OF THE SPHERES

Hopping through the woods, a rabbit was suddenly enveloped by the most sublime music he had ever heard. "Who can be singing this melody?" he wondered. "Perhaps it is a bird." He looked to the trees, but saw nothing. "No, now it sounds as if it's coming from the ground." So he searched every hole and hollow stump. Again he found nothing. Yet the delightful sound grew louder and louder as he hunted.

At last the rabbit despaired of finding its source. "Hmmmph! I've been tricked," he muttered, as he went his way. "There isn't any music at all!"

THE STING

While asleep, a man dreamed he was stung by a scorpion. As the venom spread throughout his veins, he was overwhelmed by light. When he awoke, he found himself physically paralyzed, even though the experience had been only a dream.

Because he had been a very active man, being a paralytic altered his whole style of life. He had to conduct his business from his home, by correspondence. He could not travel as he once had; his life became a "fixed point." He had to rely on friends to do many of the physical tasks he once had delighted in. But he coped admirably and continued living successfully.

Years later, he was asked by a business associate if he was bitter about his paralysis.

"Bitter?" he responded. "At first, I suppose I was—until I saw that bitterness and fear are the only things which truly paralyze a man. Soon, I came to realize that even though my body was paralyzed, my mind and spirit were not. And so I've been able to live a full and active life."

"But you are confined to your home!"

"Ah, but that has helped me discover a fuller world than I ever knew before. Because I have had to rely on friends, I have discovered a world of cooperation and affection I had never appreciated. Because I cannot move physically, I have discovered how to move in a world of goodwill and generosity I had ignored. And because I cannot travel, I have discovered a vast inner world of exotic ideas and wonderful insights I had never imagined.

"The sting of the scorpion is not so bad, my friend. It has cheated me of nothing—and has led me to chart worlds within myself I never knew existed."

42.

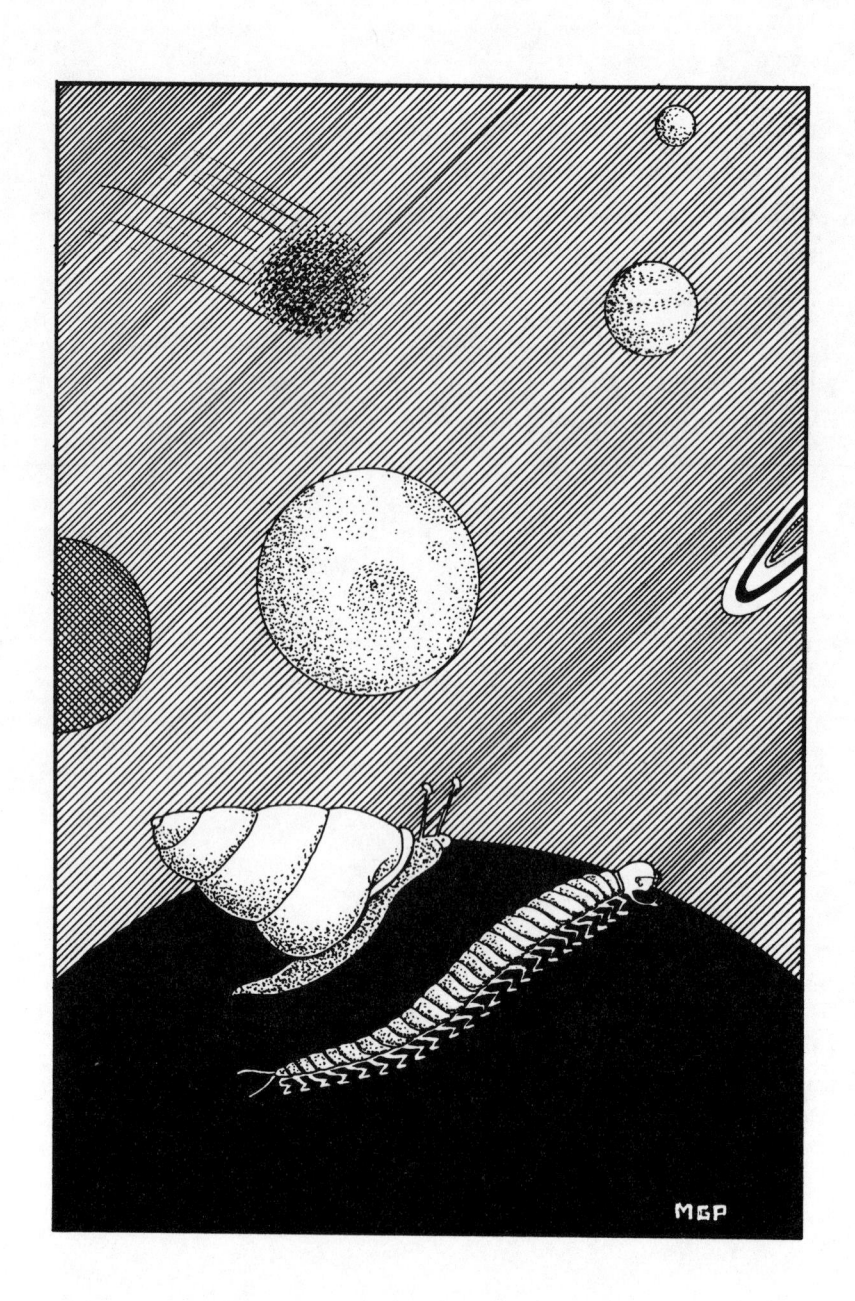

MICROCOSMIC QUESTIONS

A snail came upon a centipede in motion and asked him: "Hey, where ya goin'?"

"Where I am going," replied the centipede, "is of little importance. I am on a planet which travels millions of miles in orbit around the sun. The solar system itself is on a journey of billions of miles within the galaxy. And you ask me where I am going! How can you expect to learn anything of value asking questions like that? You should ask me where our galaxy is going. Now, there's a *real* question!"

FLUID DYNAMICS

A pure, sparkling river ran through a pine forest into a lake. But alas! The river's discontent was great, for the lake was stagnant. The river wanted something better in life than to end as green scum on the surface of a moribund lake. He told the lake: "Look at that arid land in the valley below. If you passed along some of your water, the land would bear fruit, and animals would come, and people, too." But the lake ignored the advice. So one day the river decided to bypass the lake and flow elsewhere.

It was only then the lake awoke to his error. Brimming with remorse, he wept at his loss; he sobbed and heaved until he began to shake. The convulsions of his private agony created tempestuous waves which crashed against the shoreline, eroding the banks and carving out rivulets that trickled down into the valley. The lake raved for a fortnight and a day, and then fell asleep, exhausted.

He awoke some time later to strange music. Looking down below, the lake saw birds flitting between bushes which had not grown there before. And there was grass, and crops, and a gentle wind. "Why, it must have been a miracle," he thought. "How pleasant the valley is! I wonder—could I have had anything to do with this?"

And then he glanced back to the source and saw yet another "miracle." The river had returned.

AH, FREEDOM!

A wild pig shambled up to a sty and called inside: "Brothers and sisters, we pigs have allowed ourselves to be penned up unfairly. Life is too beautiful to end up as a slice of ham next to a baked potato. Rise up and live. I know what freedom is, the freedom of the hills. The time for rebellion is now—break out of this prison and come join me."

An old sow looked up from her bed of mud. "What's your freedom worth? We're fed daily; you scavenge for food. This fence guards us against wolves; you run half a step ahead of fear both day and night. The farmer treats us well. Why should we swap our luxury for your misfortunes?"

"You speak the words of defeat," sneered the boar. "I look in this pen and I don't see pigs, I see sausages and lunchmeat, pork chops and bacon. The farmer does nothing for *you*—he feeds you to feed his stomach. You may feel cozy today, but tomorrow out comes the knife and there's the end to your comfort. Yet you can still escape—with me!"

"The knife kills quickly. Wolves aren't as considerate. Either way I end up a meal, so I think I will stay here." And saying that, the old sow rolled over in the mud.

And went back to sleep.

TOO MUCH OF A GOOD THING

Anyone will tell you he has a favorite place for relaxing, such as the sparrow who enjoyed sitting on one particular branch of one particular tree. It was a tall tree, so he had a wide view. A nice breeze cooled him off, even on the hottest of days. But most importantly, his branch was the ideal size. It was not so thin that he had trouble balancing himself, nor so thick he could not wrap his feet around it. The sparrow truly liked to curl his feet around a good, firm branch.

He liked his limb so much he invited his friends to sit on it with him, and that made the spot even better.

Now, a sparrow does not weigh very much. Even ten sparrows do not weigh a whole lot. But fifty sparrows can be a bit heavy, and that is how many friends he had. The limb began to sag. Yet the sparrow was too busy sitting on his favorite branch with all his friends to notice.

"Ah, surely this is heaven!" he chirped happily. Just then the limb snapped; the branch and all the unsuspecting birds plummeted to the ground. As the dazed friends untangled themselves from the debris, one of them replied:

"Perhaps you are right. But either we are not ready for heaven, or heaven's not ready for us."

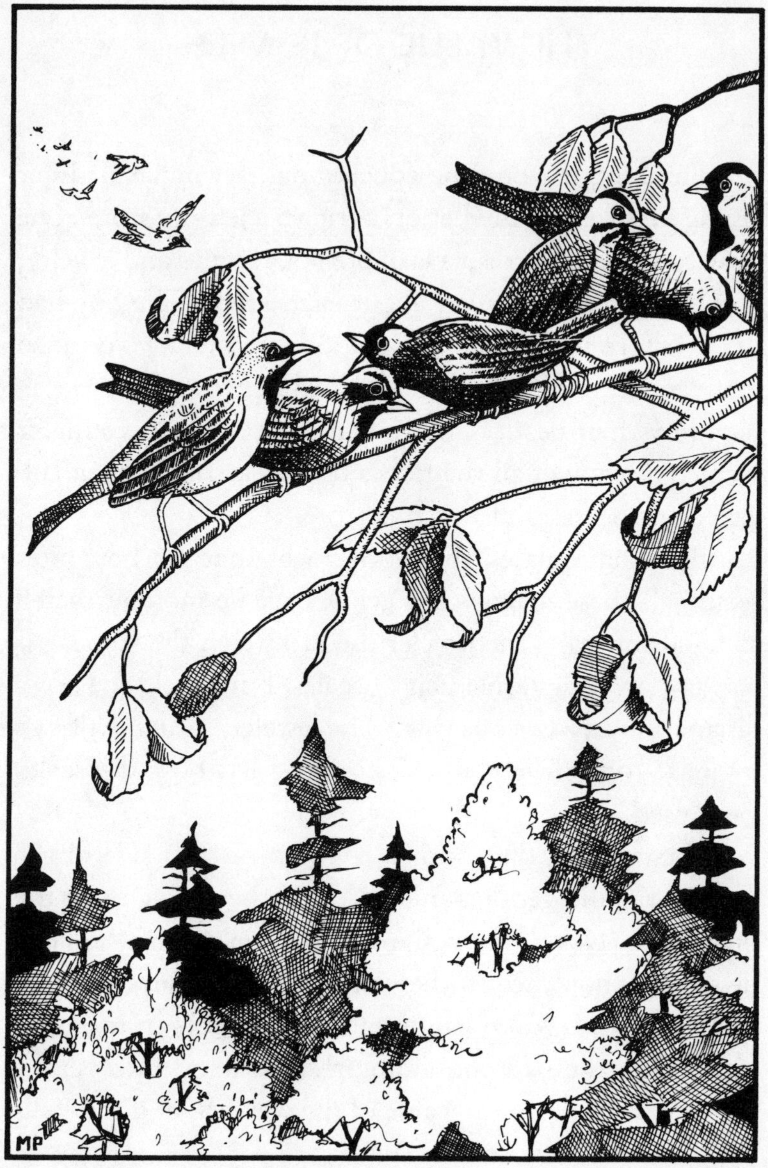

THE VALUE OF JEWELS

Thinking it would be educational, a woman had her young son accompany her on a trip to a jewelry store. She showed him all the displays of precious stones and jewelry, and explained something about each kind. The boy had never before seen so many diamonds, so much gold, or so many finely crafted items of adornment, and was fascinated by their beauty and radiance. To one so young, it seemed as though all the riches of the earth had been collected in the cases of this one store.

But what amazed the mother was that the boy, after seeing all these magnificent gems, became more attracted to a pair of scales the jeweler used to weigh the stones. It was not an exceptional pair of scales, but it held the boy's fascination in a curious way. The jeweler, seeing the boy's interest, took delight in showing the lad how the scales were used.

"I can put a diamond in the pan on this side of the scales," the old gentleman said, "and these weights in the other pan. Now, I know the value of the weights, so I can determine how heavy the diamond is by measuring it against them. When the number of weights in the right pan brings the pan containing the diamond into perfect balance, I count up the value of the weights, and that tells me how much the diamond weighs.

"Of course, I wouldn't have to use weights. I could weigh the diamond against the weight of this gold ring, or my watch, or even the coins in your pocket. That would not tell me precisely how much any of these objects weighs, but it would tell me which is the heaviest and which the lightest."

"That's neat," said the boy. "But tell me: do you always use the scales to weigh one thing *against* another? Do you ever use them to balance the one side *with* the other?"

His mother, embarrassed by the boy's impertinence, said, "Well, that's quite enough! Come along, and stop troubling the jeweler."

But the jeweler, recovering from his initial surprise, smiled. "No, Madam. Let the boy stay awhile, to teach me more about the proper value of my jewels."

SUNSPOTS

The morning sun embraced the earth, the trees and flowers basking in its gentle warmth and the rivers and lakes glistening in its light. In silent reverie the whole world thanked the sun for bringing life—all but one misshapen, crippled dwarf.

"I admit you brighten the sky," said the runt, "but I can detect spots on your crown."

"The only blotches in my glory," replied the sun, "are the reflections of detractors such as you."

51.

AMAZING GRACE

Full of bombast and brimstone, the Reverend Billy Goat was preaching at an old-time revival. "We are all tainted with sin," he shrieked. "We are not worthy of being saved, except as we believe."

He went on and on in this way—appealing to the gullible and the guilt-ridden, but making an already hot and sticky day even more unbearable for everyone else. Finally a tiny salamander, who had slinked into the revival meeting on his belly, had heard enough.

"You hypocrite," he cried in as big a voice as he could muster. "You do not believe in God—you only believe in your angry condemnations of your fellow creatures. How can we be unworthy, if God created us? How can we be lost, if God put us here on earth?"

"You wretched reptile!" bellowed the goat. "How dare you think yourself worthy. Look at you—you crawl on the ground. Worthy? Ha! Repent and be saved!"

"I crawl on the ground because I am designed to," the salamander replied with quiet dignity. "You are the one who should repent. You blaspheme the One who created me when you condemn me in this way."

With this, the Reverend Billy Goat lost his temper. "May the fire of God strike you dead!" he raged.

And lo, a bolt of lightning arced across the summer

sky, striking the ground between the Reverend Billy Goat and the salamander with an awful force. The crowd shrank back and watched with trepidation as the salamander burst into flames, then disappeared without a trace.

Even the Reverend Billy Goat was taken aback—for a moment. But he quickly recovered, and sought to make the most of the occasion—although he had not comprehended it. "As God is my witness," he declared pontifically, "this will also happen to all of you, unless you repent and follow me."

"God *is* your witness," a voice from nowhere—or perhaps from everywhere—replied. "And you are a stupid old goat. This little salamander knew his true nature, which is fire, and would not let you deny it. I have honored him by transforming him into fire before your eyes. What you have witnessed was a reward, not a punishment—a blessing, not a curse.

"You, however, do not know your true nature. Yet as I am benevolent, I shall help you discover it." And there was another flash of lightning, another roar of thunder.

"Show yourself for what you are, Billy Goat. Speak of your wisdom to the gathered throng. Teach them the way they are to follow."

But the goat could no longer talk, or even see to make his own way. He had been struck both dumb and blind— not by an act of God, but by the awesome magnitude of his own stupidity.

GOING PLACES

A kangaroo found a discarded map. "Now I can travel anywhere in the world without losing my way," she exclaimed.

Bidding her friends goodbye, she hopped off for parts unknown, the map stashed in her pouch. From time to time she spread the chart on the ground and selected a point at random with her snout: "Oh, yes—this is where I am now."

The kangaroo continued thus, until she was thoroughly lost. Finally, she sat down in despair to puzzle out her predicament. Shortly a wallaby bounced by. "What's wrong?" he inquired.

"I'm lost and can't get home," the befuddled explorer replied, "even though I've been following this map every step of the way."

Wallabies are always anxious to help. "Of course you're lost," he declared with great authority. "This map is only good for going places. It doesn't show you how to *return*."

IF ONLY

A common plow horse lived on a farm bordering a racetrack. While toiling in the fields, he could often see the thoroughbreds racing for glory. The glamour of the track filled him with aspirations to run there himself.

This horse was a strong animal from birth and unusually swift. He knew he could finish ahead of the racers, if only given the chance. But the farmer cared little how fast his horse ran—only how long he pulled the plow.

The horse resented his owner's insensitivity. "If only the jockeys could see me run!" he thought. "They'd take me from my master and race me." So, one Sunday he sneaked into the upper field. Halfway through the first race, he jumped the fence and joined the other horses on the backstretch. Running only half the race—and that without the weight of a jockey—he finished first easily. He smiled as he pulled up, expecting to be led to the winner's circle and decorated with a garland of flowers. Instead, the crowd booed, and a pair of stable boys grabbed him. Jamming a bit in his mouth, they led him off, none too gently, and returned the disgraced horse to his master.

He had run for the roses, but was forced instead to face a lesson of life: what seem to be roses often are nothing but weeds.

56.

THE STORM

A woman was tending the flowers in her garden when a fierce squall blew in from the ocean, threatening destruction. The woman was afraid that her young flowers, over which she had labored so lovingly, would be uprooted by the storm. She rose and went to meet it.

"I beg you to go around, Storm, so as not to damage these flowers in my care," she said.

"What does that matter to me?" came the reply. "I am Storm. I blow wherever I please. Your garden is no exception."

"But these are not just ordinary flowers," the woman explained. "I have cultivated them with the greatest of care. When they were still seeds in the soil, I invoked the strength of the earth to instill them with the will to grow. As they began to break through the surface of the dirt, I prayed that the warmth of the sun would fill them with aspiration. As they grew, I blessed them with the majesty of the mountains and nurtured them with beauty, love, and joy. In the evenings, I sang in harmony with the breeze blowing through the trees. And as I watered them, I taught them to worship the rainfall, for their very existence depended on it. Would you destroy life which has been nourished with a measure of your own spirit?"

Storm was touched by the woman's eloquent plea. "I

cannot go around, yet you need not be afraid for your flowers."

The woman stepped back and Storm rushed on. But as it entered her garden, it abruptly became quiet and serene. The storm stayed there the whole of the afternoon, raining softly and lovingly upon the flowers. At dusk, it regathered itself and went thundering on its way once more.

From that day forth, the flowers in the woman's garden appeared almost angelic. And the rain that fell upon them was always gentle.

THE WISDOM OF MAN

Animals being inferior to men, they tend to be susceptible to any new and exotic philosophy that happens along. Such was the case not long ago. A coyote hypothesized (in the dissertation he wrote for his doctorate in sociology) that if an animal only tried hard enough, and remained constant in his effort, he could transform himself into any other animal he desired to be.

This theory captivated the animals of the kingdom. The gophers talked of nothing except becoming weasels, the weasels vainly thought of themselves as "new age" otters, the otters encouraged their friends to think of them as foxes, the foxes mimicked the mannerisms of horses, and the horses decided they were good enough to become human beings.

Naturally, the new philosophy fast became the number one topic of conversation wherever animals gathered; books were written, it was the *only* subject for weeks on television talk shows, and instant experts appeared by the dozens, claiming to be able to teach other animals how to move up the ladder. But in spite of all the nonsense, quite a number of animals actually set out sincerely to improve themselves. And for some time the prospects were most encouraging, because each humble step an individual creature made on the ladder helped the animal kingdom as a whole to advance. At least, this is what the coyote had said.

But the philosophy failed, although not because the animals were faithless or lacked enthusiasm. Rather, the problem lay with man, who was under the impression that he was perfect—the crowning glory of evolution. Since man made no effort to become something better, the horses did not have the chance to replace him, which prevented the foxes from transforming themselves into horses, and forced the otters to be content right where they were.

You can imagine how the protozoa felt about all this.

RAISON D' ETRE

"I've half a mind to shoot you," the farmer told his no-account mutt. "You're too shiftless to hunt birds, too sleepy to be a watchdog, and too mangy to play with the children. Is it possible to justify your existence?"

"Of course," the dog protested with drowsy pride. "I have my fleas."

62.

OPEN SESAME

On the peak of a high cliff stood a large, old mansion. The people in the village below could not remember when it had been built. But they did know that fabulous parties were held day and night inside the mansion and that, by grace of an ancient treaty of friendship, they were welcome to join the festivities at any time. Still, few villagers ever took advantage of the standing invitation. Some were scared, others were shy; most simply did not care.

One night, however, a young lad from the town climbed up to the estate. He had left the village with a great sense of adventure and daring. But as he neared the palace, his confidence waned and his timidity waxed. "They do not expect me," he thought. "If I go in I will only embarrass the host and spoil the party." So he turned and fled down the hill.

Later that same evening, a second man happened to approach the mansion. But he, too, was overcome by confusion at the critical moment. "They say the door is always unlocked for us from the valley, but it is clearly closed tonight," he thought to himself. "Perhaps the host has forgotten us. No, I had better not barge in unannounced." So he sat down on the doorstep and waited, hoping the lord of the great house would come to the door and invite him in. He sat that way all night, listening to the glorious music inside the mansion but not daring to enter. At sunrise, he rose from his vigil and shuffled down the hill, disappointed.

The next night, a third man arrived at the top of the hill. He, too, saw the closed door and paused to think, "Will I really be wanted here?" But he did not retreat. Instead, he knocked on the great oaken door. When there was no answer, he said to himself: "No wonder, you fool. The music inside is so loud your gentle tap could not be heard. Try again." So he pounded on the door and then tried the knob. It turned freely and the door swung wide.

The guests inside paused to see who was at the step, and smiling happily, came over immediately to welcome the new arrival. The host himself stepped forward and cheerfully clapped the man on his shoulder, handing him a drink and signaling for more music.

"We've been waiting a long time for you," the host remarked. "But tell me: why don't more of your comrades ever come?"

THE CAT AND THE SWALLOW

One day a cat spied a swallow soaring among the tall trees. Insanely jealous that the bird could fly, the cat hailed the swallow, boasting impulsively: "I can fly faster and higher than you."

The swallow laughed. "If you can fly at all, I'll trade in my wings for galoshes and walk on water."

Goaded by this dare, the cat scrambled to the top of a nearby tree. Without hesitating, he leaped off, wildly flapping his tiny paws. "See, I can fly like you," the cat called, but his final words were lost in a screech of pain. His landing was sudden, hard, and quite clumsy.

"Poor Tom," the swallow chirped from his lofty perch. "He doesn't even *sing* like a bird."

THE STRENGTH OF THE LION

Many primitive tribes believe that if a man kills an animal and eats of its flesh, he will inherit the strengths and virtues embodied in the beast. So it was, in the ancient beginnings of time, that a party of native tribesmen set out one day to hunt the lion. Each man was filled with the anticipation of being the one who would kill the lion and become kingly in heart and strength.

On and on they marched, set on triumph, until they arrived at a grassy knoll frequented by the lions. The men hid in the bushes and waited, until their prey arrived. Even then, they did not move, waiting for the lion to lie down in the sun and fall asleep. Then they sprang forward, hurling their spears through the air. The lion was killed before he could move.

The tribesmen returned to the village victorious, rejoicing in their kill. Yet not a one of them was transformed by the death of the lion; not a one of them became kingly or virtuous.

High in the heavens, however, a transformation did occur. A new constellation of stars was formed, the constellation of the lion. Ever since, the spirit of the lion has governed the transformation of men.

67.

TOO TWO

There once was an exponent with great powers. He could square the number four and turn it into a sixteen. With a wink of his eye, six became thirty-six. Or, by simply becoming a little radical, he could humble proud eighty-one to lowly nine.

But then the exponent fell victim to illusions of grandeur. He forgot his true purpose; pouting pride crept in, and he began to yearn for independence. And so, one day he struck out on his own.

It was only then that he discovered the obvious—that he was, first and last, a number two, quite remarkable in a number of ways, but no different than all the other twos in the world.

A FUNNY THING

Wanting a centerpiece for her table, a farmer's wife went into the woods and picked an assortment of wildflowers.

"Isn't it strange?" one of the flowers remarked after they were arranged in the vase. "We've never been together before, yet we complement each other so well. What a coincidence!"

70.

ONE AND ONE IS SEVENTEEN

Back in the time before time was time, the loon was an intelligent bird—wiser than the owl and learned in such erudite subjects as Rhetoric, Elocution, and Geometry. He even dabbled in the more sublime Metaphysics. But one day he transgressed the limits of his knowledge and undertook to understand the universe.

"As far as I can see," he postulated, "something exists. But beyond the farthest ridge, is there something or is there nothing? If there is something, does it eventually end in nothing? Or if there is nothing, is it nothing forever—or does it become something else? And if nothing is sandwiched between two somethings, can it be nothing? Or is nothing something?

"I know this: I exist. I'm not nothing! Here, too, are trees and flowers and more birds. Yet, were the others here before me? What was here before them? Has something always existed? Or was there once nothing? Could something have been made from nothing?"

The more Loon thought, the more inscrutable the problem became. And the more inscrutable it became, the more unsure he felt. And the more unsure he felt, the harder he tried to think. All else became as nought—he lived, ate, and drank with one purpose: to penetrate the riddle of the universe. He abandoned his geometry and his logic; he shut himself up alone; and soon he was a frustrated, neurotic bird. Loon, the brightest of all birds, degenerated into idiocy. He wandered about in a daze, uttering weird noises and making no sense at all. The poor creature never recovered—he is still the same today.

Assuming, of course, that he actually exists.

THERE IS A SEASON

A pot was filled with water by a man, who took it to his garden to water the seeds he had just planted. The pot was quite happy to be used in this way, because the whole purpose of his being was thereby fulfilled. He derived great satisfaction from being able to carry the all-important water.

"I wonder if the man who is carrying me is sensing this same joy I am," the pot speculated, on the way back to be refilled. But no, the man did not share the pot's fulfillment at that moment: he was too busy working and making sure the garden was planted properly.

Instead, it was two months later that the man, looking out over his ripening garden, felt the spirit of fulfillment the pot had known on the first day of the work. But this time the pot, which had not been used for several weeks and was sitting in the shed, felt nothing at all.

THE CHELA

Most crabs are no more greedy than any other creature; they need food to sustain themselves, but do not prey on others maliciously. There once was a notorious exception to this rule, however—a crab who was exceedingly grasping and voracious. He could not let anything swim by without attacking it, crushing it in his pincers, and devouring it. "I *never* let go," he boasted to other crabs.

It was this very attitude which proved to be his undoing. One day he saw a movement in the water and instinctively grabbed for it. But there was actually nothing there—it had just been the movement of light upon the water—and he ended up catching himself instead, with his right claw snapping shut on the left one, even as the left claw clamped on the right.

True to form, he refused to let go, even though they were his own claws. Perhaps he did not realize he had trapped himself, but in any event, he had his prey and was too stubborn to let go of it. He slowly starved, his right pincer locked firmly on the left, and the left still clutching the right.

It was in this pathetic state that he died. As he expired, he cursed Fate for being so cruel.

Fate, sitting on her throne, responded with a groan, wondering how even a greedy crab could be so stupid.

A TASTE OF DIVINITY

Long, long ago the animals held an election to choose their leader. A baboon and a giraffe sought the honor.

The campaign was hot and furious, with the candidates kissing baby bear cubs and debating one another before the elks, the eagles, and the moose.

At one such function, the baboon announced he was divinely inspired. "Impossible!" snorted the giraffe. "The heavens have endorsed me."

"I am a prophet," the baboon countered.

To which the giraffe responded: "The gods applaud everything I do."

An old gazelle in the audience interrupted the rhetoric. "You both claim the powers of gods. I will believe it only when you have proven yourselves. Are you willing to be tested?"

Both readily accepted the challenge, so the gazelle led them—and a crowd of curious voters—to the top of a high cliff. "You jump off together," the gazelle explained. "If your boasts are true, the gods save you from crushing upon the rocks below. Are you ready?"

The candidates looked at one another apprehensively. But they had no choice. They said yes.

The gazelle counted three.

And that is how the lion was chosen king.

76.

AW, SHADDUP!

A pelican was fishing the ocean when his cousin, a blue-faced booby, happened by and hailed him. "Ho, cousin Pelican, any success?" The pelican nodded affirmatively, his mouth so full of fish he could not speak.

"Hit it lucky, eh?" the booby drawled. "Good for you. Say, y' know, I've been studyin' your technique out there, an' well, I could offer a pointer or two. Might improve your catch. First off, you're flyin' too high 'bove the water. Makes it hard t' see the fish—an' if ya can't see 'em, ya can't catch 'em, I always say. An' as ya begin your dive, Cousin, you're hesitatin'. Hesitatin' like that gives the fish a chance to 'scape 'neath the surface. An' then a third thing—" And the blue-faced booby babbled on.

Finally, the pelican finished his meal. Turning smugly to his cousin, he asked: "Tell me, brother Booby, have you caught *your* breakfast yet?"

The blue-faced booby's blue face paled. "Uh, well...y' see, the current's runnin' the wrong way, an' the wind is awful strong, an' the stars are in bad signs, an' my timin's a little off—"

"Well, if you're hungry from all that talking," the pelican interrupted, "you're welcome to my leavings."

And he flew away.

THE PROCESSION OF MAN

Along one side of the forest ran a long, curving road, not a superhighway for speeding automobiles but a footpath on which many men traveled. The animals never ventured near the path; they were content within the confines of the woods. But one old buzzard built her nest in a tall tree on the outer edge of the forest, and from her vantage point could daily watch the procession of men on the trail.

And a strange march it was. The bird was completely puzzled by it, unable to perceive the meaning of the men's actions. A few walked the road with a steady pace, confident in their abilities and sure of their goal. Once or twice she had seen a man who fairly galloped up the trail.

Others plodded very slowly, as if each step was painful and heavy. But most of the men had simply stopped, unslung their packs, and slumped alongside the road—and often in the middle of the road, forcing those following to step over. Many rested that way for days and days—the buzzard knew not how many—before gathering strength to reshoulder their packs again. A number had not moved for as long as the old bird had observed the road. And for each who collapsed under his load, the burden had doubled by the time he set out again on the trail.

At last, the buzzard's curiosity got the best of her, and

79.

she flew over to inspect the strange men more closely. She landed by one of the newly-fallen and asked, "Why have you stopped walking?"

"I'm at the end of the line," came the gasping answer.

"But you aren't," the buzzard replied. "There are still miles of road ahead."

"This looks like the peak to me."

"You can't see around the bends. From my perch in the trees, I can look at what lies ahead."

"I'm more satisfied right where I am," the man said. "And what's more, I don't believe you—this *is* the top. It must be—look at all the others resting here, too." And there was a large crowd, in fact.

Suddenly, one of the men who had been resting stood up, hoisted his burden, and trudged off once more. The buzzard flew over and asked, "Why are you starting out again?"

"There's more trail ahead."

"But how can you see around the bend, when that other man cannot?"

"I don't know," he said. "I couldn't when I stopped, but I can now." And he disappeared around a corner of rock.

More baffled than before, the buzzard crossed over to one of the men who had been resting for as long as she had been watching the road. "What are you waiting for?"

No answer came.

"Can't you see this isn't the end of the road?"
Still nothing.
"I suppose you think that this is the summit, that this is what you've been striving for, that you can relax forever without a care."

But he thought no such thought, for he was dead.

Dead on the road, and not even the buzzard could tell.

THE TREE IN THE GARDEN

The Town told the man he would receive electric power. The man told himself how fortunate he was. Then the Town informed him the tree in the garden would be cut down. It interfered with the wires.

"You can't cut down that tree," the man replied.

"Why not?" the Town demanded.

"My father planted it the day I was born. I played in its shade as a child. I proposed to my wife under its branches. I love that tree."

"Mere sentimentality," the Town replied.

"It is not!" the man objected. "This tree is part of me; it is rooted in my very marrow. Don't you understand?"

The Town did, but did not show it. "We cannot install the wires while that tree stands."

"Then I don't want electricity," the man said.

"Don't be silly," the Town chided. "Of course you want electricity. Everyone wants electricity."

"No!" the man cried. "I won't allow it!"

And he didn't. Which is a shame, for had the man seen the light, he would have known that the light is good.

A STRANGE THING

There once were two axes. One was very self-centered, always complaining about how hard life was and trying to get out of work. He bitterly resented having his brains knocked out every day, by being struck time after time against hard wood. When it was time to be sharpened, he almost fainted as his owner spit on him to moisten his edge, and thought it sheer torture to be honed on the whetstone. He would have much preferred to remain dull—and in truth, many of his friends thought he was.

The other axe was very well balanced. He understood his purpose and delighted in being of service to mankind. He knew that an occasional bit of friction and steady use were part of his life, but he accepted these conditions joyfully, rather than complain about them. He styled himself as a "cutting edge" and thought about the homes which were built from the wood he cut, the furniture that was handcrafted, and the people who were warmed by the firewood he had felled. His life was full of satisfaction and a sense of contribution.

It is not hard to guess which axe a teller of fables would choose to fell his trees. But the strange thing is that these two axes belonged to the same woodsman—who used them both every day, without favoring the one over the other.

84.

THE PANIC

A tiny mouse peered up through the tall grasses and beheld a gigantic hippopotamus. The mouse had never seen—had not even imagined—such a large animal before. The poor thing ran back to his family, screaming:

"Monster! Monster! It is the end of the world!" And he collapsed and expired from fright.

The testimony of a dead mouse can never be doubted. So the mice panicked and began running helter-skelter. As they fled, they were seen by rabbits and squirrels and groundhogs, who asked what was happening.

"It's the end of the world, that's all!" the mice shouted back. "A huge monster is running loose and destroying everything!"

At such times of obvious international crisis, not a moment can be wasted. The rabbits and squirrels and groundhogs immediately joined the mice in their mad dash. They in turn were seen by deer and bears and horses, who asked why everyone was running so fast. "A monster is annihilating the earth," someone cried. Recognizing the socio-economic implications of the situation, the deer and bears and horses took to their heels as well.

Finally the wild stampede thundered past a group of hippos wallowing in a shallow mudhole. "What's wrong?" asked a sleepy hippo. "A giant is on the loose and is going to destroy us all!" a horse replied breathlessly. "Run, or you shall be killed!"

The hippos looked lazily at one another. They were not entirely sure they *could* run. But without a doubt, the world was in great jeopardy: *something* had to be done. And so, with great effort, they crawled out of the mudhole and waddled off with the rest, to meet their unknown fate.

A FALSE PRETENSION

A wire fence dividing two fields felt important because he kept the animals to his south out of the corn to his north. But soon dogs had tunneled underneath him, the horses had jumped over him, and the bulls had trampled him underfoot.

88.

SNAKEBITTEN

A reader of omens sat by his modest pile of embers, warming his hands against the cold bite of early morning. A woodcutter, on his way to the forest, paused by the soothsayer's fire.

"Tell me, Father, what's in store for today?"

The prophet gazed into the glowing coals. "You shall be struck by a viper before sundown."

The woodcutter laughed. "You can tell tales better than that, Father. There aren't any poisonous snakes in these woods." And he headed off to his day's chores.

That evening the woodsman returned from the forest, lugging a huge bundle of logs he had sawn during the day. Stopping by the seer's fire, he unslung his pack and said good-naturedly: "The sun is setting even now, Father, and your viper has not bitten me."

The reader of omens looked up from his sputtering fire. "Good fortune has smiled on you. Waste no time: thank the heavens for your deliverance. Build a fire of sacrifice here by my hut."

"Oh-ho," the woodsman cried. "Now I understand your false words—you hope to trick me out of my day's labor of wood. I'll have none of that, Cheat."

The prophet replied evenly: "Call me what you wish, but I will tell you once more: build the fire. For the serpent is trapped in your bundle, and you shall be bitten if you do not burn it whole."

The stubborn woodcutter refused to believe. "I will prove you wrong, Father," he answered, unlashing the load. But as he loosened the logs, he uncovered the viper, which struck him on the hand. The woodsman pulled the snake off his wrist and flung the reptile into the fire at the feet of the prophet.

"Father, Father: forgive my disbelief," cried the man. "How bad is the bite—will I die?"

The reader of omens watched his fire feed on the writhing serpent. "No, the bite is not fatal," he said. "The snake always spares the unbeliever."

SHHH...

A doe and her fawn paused on a knoll overlooking a gently-flowing stream. "Look at this pleasant brook, my son, which refreshes the whole valley yet flows without a noise. Be like this stream: assist your neighbors at every turn, but quietly."

92.

THE BULL'S CROWN

Bulls can be as moody as they look. One in particular became quite sullen, because he did not like his reputation among the other animals. He wanted to be liked, but was feared; he wanted to be respected, but was avoided. He concluded it must be his horns. "It's these horns which make them afraid of me," he thought. "Oh, if only I could be rid of them!" He grew quite desperate and tried to tear them off, ramming the horns against trees and fences, but all he managed to do was give himself a very bad headache.

The moon saw his anguish and spoke to him. "Why are you so upset with your horns?" she inquired.

"They are misshapen and fearful," said the bull.

"Nonsense," cried the moon. "They are shaped like a crescent, just as I am. You carry on the top of your head a very proud heritage—a piece of heaven, come to earth. You should wear it with dignity."

"If it is a piece of heaven, come to earth," rebutted the bull, "why is everyone so afraid of me?"

"Not everyone is," the moon replied quietly. "You exaggerate these fears. The mountains and valleys do not fear you; neither do the stars or the sun. Not even the clouds, as puffy as they are, run from you. Only those who do not see me in the horns on your head fear you."

"Why have you never told me this before?" asked the bull, feeling somewhat better about himself.

"It's something you should have been able to discover on your own," said the moon. "You wear the sign of the moon as a crown—but you are designed to live the life of the bull."

TALES OF LONG AGO

Aesop listened restlessly as a fellow Greek harangued hour after hour against the excesses of Athenian youth—how their immorality and disrespect for the ways of their elders would surely topple the pillars of democracy if left unchecked. At last the orator paused and turned to the famous story teller. "Would you not agree with me, wise Aesop?"

The fabulist's answer was terse. "Examples abound in the animal world of parents eating their young," he said, "but I cannot think of a single example of the reverse."

ROCK SEQUITER

A dynamite explosion sent a tremendous mass of dirt and stone flying in all directions. Hurtling through the air, one good-sized boulder reflected to himself: "This flying is marvelous! When I land, I must be sure to set up a school and teach other rocks how to do it, too."

THE MASTERPIECE

A jackass entered an art contest held by the animals in his district. As he registered, he was asked what medium he would be working in. "Sculpture," he replied. The registrar—a raccoon—then asked him what materials he would be using in his sculpture.

"Water," said the jackass.

The raccoon was astounded. "Water? I've never heard of anyone making a sculpture of water. It can't be done!"

"That's what you say!" said the jackass, and he went over to the work area he had been assigned.

Later, the judges stopped by and found the jackass sitting on the ground, with no sculpture. He had managed to spill all his water about him. The judges chuckled at this sight and decided to humor the jackass. "How's the sculpture coming?" they asked.

"I'm finished," the jackass said.

"And what do you call your masterpiece?" asked one of the judges, a big, burly bear who could hardly keep from laughing.

"Tears shed by the loser in an art show," said the jackass solemnly.

He was voted the winner unanimously.

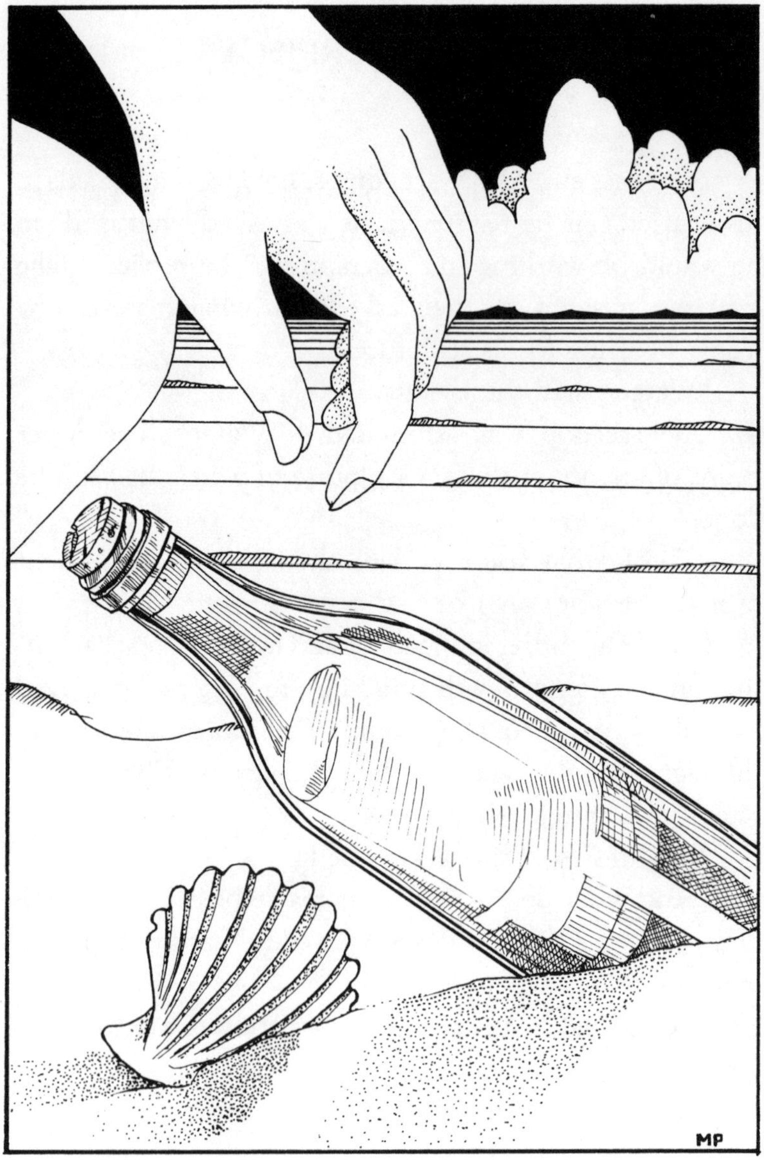
MP

THE SECRET

Walking on a beach, a man found a bottle lying in the sand. As he stopped to pick it up, a voice whispered in his ear: "This bottle contains the secret of life."

Upon hearing this, the man decided to discover the secret. So he uncorked the bottle, thinking it might contain a magic elixir he could drink and become all-knowing. But the bottle was empty.

Then he thought, "Perhaps the bottle contains a genie who can tell me the secret—and grant me some wishes besides." So he tried rubbing the side of the bottle and chanting a few Oriental slogans, but nothing happened.

Finally, having become quite frustrated, he smashed the bottle on a rock. It was then he discovered there had been a note inside. The man picked it up and read it.

"Here is the secret of life," the note said. "The bottle is *whole*."

THE LEADER OF THE FLOCK

The instinct of sheep is strong and powerful; it binds them together in the common flock. But other impulses even stronger than instinct do arise. So it was with one young sheep, who gradually became convinced that he must leave the flock to pursue his own destiny.

The thought of striking out on his own terrified him, for he knew not what awaited him, but something stronger than terror led him on. The prospect of leaving the flock saddened him, but something greater than sadness reassured him that he must. And so, one night as the rest of the flock slept, he slipped away.

He knew not where to go, but followed the impulse within him as best he could. It led him through forests and across plains, close to villages and out into the most desolate regions. He frequently encountered danger, and hardly a day went by that he did not doubt the wisdom of his decision to leave.

When he slept, he dreamed of the flock. At first, they gently called him to return. In later dreams, they became more threatening, accusing him of abandoning them and angrily attacking him. But the ram remained resolute, awakening from his dreams bleating, "I *must* do this." He felt terrible to be apart from the flock, but pressed on.

At last, he came to a valley which was different from

the others he had traveled through; the fragrance of the flowers was most exotic, as though tended by angels, and the birds sang with unrestrained joy. The whole valley seemed to radiate light. He hesitated to enter, but as he did, his impulse to wander and explore departed. He felt a great sense of release and sank into a deep and peaceful slumber.

When he awoke, the sheep was startled to find, there in the valley of his discovery, the rest of his flock. "Did you follow me here to force me to come back?" he asked.

"No," they responded, "we followed you because you led the way to a much better home, to a new beginning. We accept you now as leader of the flock."

"But you attacked me in my dreams."

"We did not share your vision, and were afraid. Now we know you are right. Let us join you here."

The sheep smiled and cried with delight, happy to be one with the flock again. He knew, at that moment, that he had been guided, and his friends had been drawn, by the deepest instinct of all: the instinct to follow a genuine purpose.

THE GREY-EYED GLACK

Few have heard of the grey-eyed glack, a bird of bright pink feathers and charcoal grey eyes. There is a good reason: the grey-eyed glack is extinct. It is a curious story.

It happened that the last of the grey-eyed glacks knew he was the last of the grey-eyed glacks, because he could not find a female grey-eyed glack. This might have been an oversight, but it can be assumed he tried mighty hard.

As if the lack of a female glack were not trouble enough, the last of the line was weighed down by the awful historical perspective of his situation. He felt it incumbent upon himself to preserve the identity of grey-eyed glacks for all time. But he did not know how.

This dilemma worried him a lot. He tried imprinting his foot in sand, but the rain and wind erased it. He tried teaching other birds the song of the glack, but they were not interested.

The time finally came for the last of the grey-eyed glacks to leave this life. Yet even as he lay on his deathbed, the idea he had been awaiting came. He called to his side his best friend.

"I'm the last of my species," he breathed. "You can perpetuate yourself through your children—I cannot. Promise me one thing, my friend. Tell your children there once existed a grey-eyed glack, and you knew the last of the kind. Tell them what I looked like, and make them swear to tell their children the same. Will you do that for me?"

His friend was caught up in the solemnity of the moment. "Of course I will," he said, emotion tensing his voice. "You will be remembered throughout all time—or I am not the Great Auk."

THE HOUR GLASS

An owl who said very little, and was consequently considered very wise, possessed an hour glass nearly as large as himself. Each night he sat in his tree watching by moonlight as the sands fell. From time to time he called out the hour, and although the other birds did not understand him, they held their friend in great awe.

Early one evening a young owl flew over to visit the timekeeper. "What's so important about time?" the youth inquired.

"It has taught me a lesson you can profit from," the old owl answered. "The sands in this glass are not time, but a metaphor of time. The grains falling now are the present; they are full of action, like yourself. The sands on top are moments yet to come, the sands below are moments past.

"But mark you well," the owl proceeded, inverting the instrument, "the glass is reversed every hour. The sands of the past become the sands of the future once more, although they do not necessarily fall in the same sequence."

"So?"

"So, never worry about the future, for you can always find it recorded in the past. And never bemoan the past, for it shall be repeated countless times in the future."

105.

ABOUT THE AUTHOR

Carl Japikse has been writing fables since his days at Dartmouth College, where he encountered a wide variety of animals. He has worked for several newspapers, including *The Wall Street Journal*. In the early 1970's, he left journalism to pursue his current interests: teaching, writing, and lecturing. He is the developer of *The Enlightened Management Seminar* and co-author, with Robert Leichtman, M.D. of a number of books on personal growth:

Active Meditation: The Western Tradition
The Art of Living
The Life of Spirit

To Mr. Japikse, a good fable is entertaining, filled with inner meaning, and short. He also says that while any resemblance between animals in these fables and animals the reader may know is coincidental and unintentional, he will be happy to take credit for it anyway.

He and his wife Rose reside in Columbus, Ohio.

ABOUT THE ARTIST

A dot once appeared to Mark Peyton on a sheet of paper and said, "Push me." He pushed, and his first line was drawn. Today, the same dot performs internationally.